Lots of the little animals are taking part in the Thistletown Talent Show, but poor Willow isn't feeling very well. What can be the matter, and will she feel better in time for the performance?
You'll have to read the story to find out!

For BB the duck — J.C.

OXFORD
UNIVERSITY PRESS

Great Clarendon Street, Oxford OX2 6DP
Oxford University Press is a department of the University of Oxford.
It furthers the University's objective of excellence in research, scholarship,
and education by publishing worldwide

Text © Jane Clarke and Oxford University Press 2016
Illustrations © Oxford University Press 2016

Cover artwork: Richard Byrne
Cover photographs: Tony Campbell, Tsekhmister,
Pakhnyushchy/Shutterstock.com
Inside artwork: Dynamo
All animal images from Shutterstock
With thanks to Christopher Tancock for advising on the first aid

The moral rights of the author/illustrator have been asserted

Database right Oxford University Press (maker)

First published in 2016

British Library Cataloguing in Publication Data

Data available

ISBN: 978-0-19-274335-0 (paperback)

2 4 6 8 10 9 7 5 3 1

Printed in China
Paper used in the production of this book is a natural,
recyclable product made from wood grown in sustainable forests.
The manufacturing process conforms to the environmental
regulations of the country of origin.

Dr KittyCat

is ready to rescue

Willow the Duckling

Jane Clarke

OXFORD
UNIVERSITY PRESS

Chapter One

Peanut peeped out of the window of Dr KittyCat's clinic. A long line of young animals was waiting at the door.

'We're going to be busy this morning,' he squeaked. 'It looks as if every little animal in Thistletown has come to be vaccinated against fur and feather flu!'

'Purr-fect,' Dr KittyCat purred happily. 'No one wants to get flu.'

'Especially now,' Peanut agreed. 'It's the Thistletown Talent Show in ten days.'

'I'm looking forward to seeing everyone's acts,' Dr KittyCat meowed, taking a box from the supplies cupboard and handing it to Peanut. 'There are some very talented animals in Thistletown.'

Peanut opened the box. It was full of individually wrapped plastic tubes with plungers. Each little tube was filled with the same amount of liquid.

'Each tube contains exactly the right dose of the vaccine,' Dr KittyCat told him as she unwrapped one.

'I've already given myself the vaccination. Now it's your turn, Peanut. I'll vaccinate you before we open the clinic.'

Peanut's ears twitched.

'Eek!' he squeaked. 'I don't like injections!' His whiskers quivered.

'Don't panic, Peanut,' Dr KittyCat meowed. 'The new vaccine for fur and feather flu isn't an injection. It's a nose spray. The plunger pumps a mist of

vaccine into your nostril. It will be
over in a whisker.'

Peanut sat very still as
Dr KittyCat gently placed the end of
the tube in his nostril and pushed the
plunger with her soft paw. It didn't
hurt at all.

'That was nothing,' he said, whiffling
his whiskers. 'It just felt a bit tickly.'

'Well done,' Dr KittyCat meowed.
'Now, you can reassure our patients.
It's time to open the clinic.'

Peanut scampered to the door.
'Come in!' he told the young animals
who were waiting. 'The flu vaccine is
a nose spray. It doesn't hurt at all.'

Sage the owlet was first in line.
She blinked her big eyes at them.

'Don't worry,' Peanut told her.
'You're safe in our paws.'

'I'm not worried,' Sage hooted.
'But why do I need to take medicine
when I'm not ill?'

'Fur and feather flu is caused by a type of germ called a virus,' Dr KittyCat explained. 'Coughs and sneezes release virus germs into the air. A vaccine is a sort of medicine that helps your body fight off the virus before it can make you poorly.'

'And by having the vaccine, you help protect everyone in Thistletown, because you won't get the virus and pass it on to anyone else,' Peanut added.

'I see.' Sage nodded her head up and down. She stood patiently as Dr KittyCat gently squirted a dose of vaccine into Sage's nostrils at the top of her beak.

'Well done!' Dr KittyCat meowed.

Peanut handed Sage a sticker with 'I was a purr-fect patient for Dr KittyCat' on it.

I was a purr-fect patient for Dr KittyCat!

'Thanks,' Sage said. 'I don't want to catch flu. I'm the host for the Thistletown Talent Show. I'm learning lots of jokes. It will be a hoot!'

'I'm sure it will,' Dr KittyCat laughed.

'I'm going to perform some magic tricks,' Clover the bunny told them as he stepped up and tilted his furry nose for Dr KittyCat. 'It takes lots of practice.'

'I've decided to sing a song,' Posy

the puppy woofed.

    'And I'm doing a web foot waltz,'
Willow the duckling quacked excitedly.
'It's really difficult!'

There was a buzz of chatter in the clinic as all the little animals talked excitedly about the acts they were going to perform at the show.

Soon, everyone had been vaccinated. Peanut took out Dr KittyCat's *Furry First-aid Book*.

'These little animals don't need to worry about getting flu,' he commented as he wrote their names in the book.

'That's good to know,' Dr KittyCat meowed as she reached in her bag for her knitting. 'I'd hate to think of

anyone missing the talent show. They're so excited about their performances.'

I've never performed on stage, Peanut thought dreamily. *I wonder what it feels like?* He closed his eyes and imagined himself singing and dancing in the spotlight.

'It will be amazing!' he squeaked.
'I can't wait to see the show!'

Chapter Two

On the afternoon of the Thistletown
Talent Show, Peanut and Dr KittyCat
were in the clinic, working at their desks.
Peanut was reading aloud from
Dr KittyCat's *Furry First-aid Book*.

'The symptoms of fur and feather
flu are sore throat, hoarseness, cough,
fever, muscular tingles and aches,' he

read. He closed the
book. 'It sounds really
nasty,' he squeaked.
'I hope we don't have an
outbreak in Thistletown.
What if it spreads as quickly
as pawpox does?'

'Don't panic, Peanut,' Dr KittyCat
meowed. 'We haven't seen
any cases of the flu since
we gave the animals
the vaccine.' She
opened her flowery
doctor's bag and
began to check
the contents.

'Scissors, syringe, medicines, ointments, instant cool packs, paw-cleansing gel and wipes,' she murmured. 'Stethoscope, opthalmoscope, thermometer, tweezers, bandages, gauze, sticking plasters, surgical head lamp, magnifying glass, dental mirror . . .

tongue depressor, lozenges, pastilles and reward stickers. Everything is where it should be,' Dr KittyCat declared. 'If there's an emergency at the performance tonight, we'll be ready to rescue.' She took out her knitting.

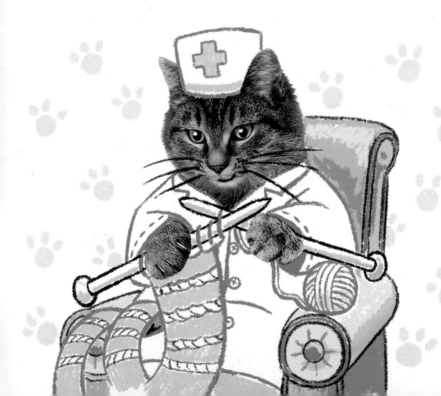

Peanut
glanced at it.
It was long and
thin and stripy.
Dr KittyCat was
knitting a little
scarf. *I wouldn't
mind if that was*
for me, he thought. *I need a new scarf for*
the winter . . .

The telephone on his desk began
to ring.

Peanut grabbed the handset.

'Dr KittyCat's clinic. How can we
help?' he asked, twirling the telephone
cord around his paw.

'Eek!' he squeaked. 'It's Thistletown Theatre,' he told Dr KittyCat. 'Willow's collapsed on stage at the final rehearsal. She's snuffling and gasping. It sounds like fur and feather flu! They'll have to call off tonight's show!'

'Don't panic, Peanut,' Dr KittyCat said as she took the phone.

'Keep Willow calm and quiet,' she purred reassuringly. 'We'll be there in a whisker!'

She replaced the handset on its cradle.

'You should try to keep calm and quiet, too, Peanut,' she told him as she picked up her flowery doctor's bag.

'I'll try!' Peanut gripped

Dr KittyCat's *Furry First-aid Book* tightly between his paws as they hurried to the vanbulance.

Their brightly painted van was parked outside the clinic. Peanut and Dr KittyCat jumped in and swished their tails out of the way of the doors. They clipped on their seatbelts.

'Ready to rescue?' Dr KittyCat meowed, grabbing hold of the steering wheel.

'Ready to rescue!' Peanut slammed his paw on the button on the dashboard that turned on the siren.

Nee-nah! Nee-nah! Nee-nah!

The vanbulance sped off, juddering
and bumping over the timber bridge.

'Eek!' Peanut squeaked, as he
bounced up and down on his seat.

'Eek!' he squealed again as the vanbulance rounded Duckpond Bend on two wheels.

Dr KittyCat put her paw on the accelerator.

Vroom! The vanbulance shot down the narrow country lane. *Dr KittyCat thinks she's a racing driver,* Peanut thought, closing his eyes. His whiskers started to quiver.

'Eek!' he shrieked. His heart was thumping and his paws felt all clammy.

'You're panicking, Peanut,'
Dr KittyCat murmured. 'You need to
learn to calm down and relax.'

'How?' Peanut squeaked. 'I take
a deep breath sometimes and that
seems to help a bit, but not for long.'

'Breathing exercises are very
helpful,' Dr KittyCat meowed, 'but you
need to concentrate and keep repeating
them. Ready?'

Peanut nodded.

'Breathe in slowly and deeply
through your nose, as if you're
breathing in the scent of something
lovely,' Dr KittyCat purred. 'What's
your favourite smell?'

'Cheese,' squeaked Peanut. 'But there are so many different cheesy smells!'

'Just choose one,' Dr KittyCat told him. 'How about Emmental?'

'I love that sort of holey Swiss

cheese,' Peanut sighed. 'It smells warm, and buttery and nutty . . .'

'Concentrate on that,' Dr KittyCat meowed encouragingly. 'Breathe in slowly and breathe out slowly and smoothly.'

Peanut breathed out a long sigh.

'Slower, as if you're blowing out a hundred candles on your birthday cake,' Dr KittyCat went on.

'But I don't have a hundred candles on my birthday cake,' Peanut squeaked. 'I'm not that old!'

'Pretend,' Dr KittyCat instructed. Peanut pursed his lips and blew out very slowly.

'Well done,' purred Dr KittyCat. 'Concentrate on breathing slowly and deeply in and out. If you keep on doing that, you'll soon feel calmer.'

Peanut concentrated hard on his breathing. It was impossible to think about that and worry about Dr KittyCat's driving. He could feel his heartbeat gradually slow down and his whiskers stop twitching.

'It's working,' he smiled, opening his eyes.

'Just in time,' Dr KittyCat

meowed. 'We're here!'

She slammed her feet on the brakes and the vanbulance screeched to a halt outside Thistletown Theatre.

Billy the budgie, who worked at the theatre, rushed out to meet them.

'Willow says her wings feel all tingly,' he cheeped.

'Eek!' Peanut squeaked. 'That's one of the symptoms of fur and feather flu . . .'

'Don't panic, Peanut,' he told himself. He took two deep slow breaths in and out and opened Dr KittyCat's *Furry First-aid Book* and checked his notes.

'Willow's name's in the book!' he exclaimed. 'She came to the clinic and had her vaccination. So, she can't have fur and feather flu. Whatever is going on?'

'Let's find out!' Dr KittyCat meowed.

'We're here now,' Dr KittyCat meowed reassuringly. 'Can you tell us what's wrong?'

Willow poked her head out from under her wing. She was shuddering so much her feathers were quivering.

'She's snuffling and gasping too much to quack,' Billy told them.

Dr KittyCat opened her doctor's bag. 'Thank you for your help,' she told the little animals. 'I'd like everyone to leave the stage, now. Peanut and I will find out what's the matter with Willow, and make it better.'

The little animals jumped down from the stage.

Dr KittyCat turned to the poorly duckling.

'Willow, I'm going to make sure nothing's getting in the way of your breathing,' she said. 'Can you stand very still and open your beak?'

Willow nodded.

Dr KittyCat could see that Willow's airway was clear. So then she looked, listened, and felt to make sure the little duckling was breathing normally.

'I need to listen to your chest, now . . .'

Peanut handed her the stethoscope.

'I can't hear any wheezing,' Dr KittyCat commented, 'so you're not having an asthma attack . . .'

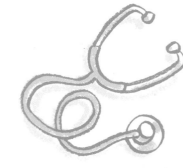

Peanut watched as Dr KittyCat checked Willow over to make sure she wasn't in shock. 'It's hot in the spotlight, but your feet do feel a little cold and clammy . . .' she remarked.

'Like my paws when you were driving,' Peanut murmured.

Dr KittyCat looked up. 'You may be on to something, Peanut,' she told him. She turned back to the duckling.

'Do your wings still feel tingly?'
she asked.

Willow shook her head.

'Good.' Dr KittyCat smiled.
'You're beginning to feel better.
Let's move you out of the spotlight.'

Peanut helped Dr KittyCat
move the fluffy duckling to the back
of the stage.

'Willow will be much more
comfortable here,' Dr KittyCat
meowed. 'I'll stay and look after her.
You go and ask the others exactly
what happened.'

Peanut hopped off the stage.
The little animals gathered round him.

'Will Willow be all right?'
Posy woofed anxiously.

'Yes,' Peanut reassured them.
'She's feeling a bit better already, but
she still can't quack. Dr KittyCat needs
to know exactly what happened, so
I need you to answer some questions.

Who can tell me when Willow started to feel poorly?'

There was a pause as all the little animals thought hard.

'I was standing behind Willow in the line waiting to go up on stage,' Pumpkin the hamster said. 'She was shuffling about a long time before her turn. I asked her what was wrong and she said she had butterflies in her tummy. I told her that I did, too.'

'So did I!' whistled Nutmeg the guinea pig.

'Who was in front of Willow?' Peanut asked.

'Me!' Posy wagged her tail at Peanut.

'How did Willow seem to you?'
Peanut asked the little puppy.

'She whispered that her heart
was thumping and she felt really
nervous,' Posy woofed. 'Which was
a bit like how I felt.'

Clover piped up,
'I was on stage doing my
magic act and I could
hear her snuffling from
there!'

'It was Posy's turn
after Clover's,' Pumpkin
told Peanut. 'All through the song
Willow was shuffling from foot to foot.
She couldn't keep still.'

'So what happened when it was Willow's turn?' Peanut squeaked.

'She looked like she was frozen to the spot,' Sage hooted. 'I had to tell her to get up on the stage and dance. Then . . . when the spotlight shone on her, she started to gasp and collapsed in a heap. We called you straight away!'

'Thank you,' Peanut squeaked. 'You've all been very helpful. I'll tell Dr KittyCat.' He scampered to the back of the stage and relayed all the information he'd been given.

'It sounds as if Willow has had a very bad case of stage fright,' Dr KittyCat meowed thoughtfully.

'Would that cause all of her symptoms?' Peanut asked.

'Stage fright on its own wouldn't make her feet go clammy and her wings tingle,' Dr KittyCat meowed. 'But a panic attack would . . . I think Willow has had a panic attack brought on by acute stage fright.'

'How do you feel now?' she asked Willow.

'Much better,' the duckling quacked softly.

'Can you tell us how you felt when you were in the spotlight?' Dr KittyCat asked her gently.

'I was so afraid!' Willow quacked.

'My heart was thumping so hard I couldn't breathe and my knees knocked together and my feathers shook all over. Then the room started spinning. I thought I was going to choke!'

'Poor Willow, you definitely had a panic attack,' Dr KittyCat murmured sympathetically. 'A panic attack feels very, very scary, but it's all over now.'

'It was horrid!' Willow quacked. 'I don't think I'll ever dare to get on stage again.' Her feathers drooped. 'I'll miss the talent show, and I practised so hard for it. It took me ages to learn my dance.'

'It doesn't take long to learn to keep calm and relax so you can stop it happening again,' Dr KittyCat reassured her. 'One of the best ways is to do a deep breathing exercise—like the one I taught you, Peanut.'

'It really helps!' Peanut squeaked. 'Maybe you should teach it to everyone. A lot of the little animals are nervous about their performances tonight.'

'That's a good idea,' Dr KittyCat meowed.

Peanut went to the front of the stage and called down to the little animals.

'Willow's better now,' he told them. 'She had a nasty panic attack.'

'What's a panic attack?' whistled Nutmeg.

'Like a very bad attack of stage fright only much, much worse,' Peanut explained.

A murmur of sympathy echoed round the hall.

'It's natural to feel a bit nervous about going on stage tonight,' Peanut squeaked. 'Dr KittyCat is going to share an exercise to help everyone to keep calm and relax.'

Peanut led Willow down from the stage and into the audience as Dr KittyCat stepped into the spotlight.

'You can do this exercise standing up in an emergency,' Dr KittyCat announced, 'but when you practise it, it's best to be relaxed, so everyone sit down, or lie down . . .' She waited for them to get comfortable. 'Close your eyes if you like.'

Peanut lay down quietly on the floor.

'Now, breathe in slowly and deeply through your nose,' she instructed. 'As if you're smelling something lovely . . .'

'Like cheese,' Peanut squeaked.

'Or water weed,' Willow quacked.

'Or bones!' Posy woofed.

'The smell you choose will be

different for everyone,' Dr KittyCat meowed calmly. 'Now, breathe out slowly through your mouth . . .'

'As if you're blowing out a hundred candles on a birthday cake,' Peanut added.

'Or pretend you're blowing a stream of bubbles, or blowing up a balloon,' Dr KittyCat meowed. 'Keep on breathing slowly in and out, and imagine you're in your favourite place, doing your favourite thing . . .'

'I'm nibbling my way through a field of dandelions,' Nutmeg whistled.

'I'm on a tennis court, running after all the balls,' Posy woofed.

'I'm paddling down a crystal-clear stream,' Willow quacked.

Dr KittyCat dropped her voice. 'Keep breathing slowly and deeply and concentrate on what you can see, what you can hear, and what you can smell . . .' she meowed softly.

Peanut closed his eyes. It was
easy to imagine he was in a cheese
shop, inhaling the delicious aromas of
a hundred different sorts of cheese. *I'll
sample them one by one,* he thought,
*starting with this creamy blue cheese
that smells of stinky socks . . .*

'Peanut's dribbling!' Sage hooted.

Peanut jumped to his feet and wiped his mouth with the back of his paw.

'Try to concentrate on what you're doing, not on what the others are doing,' Dr KittyCat told them as Peanut lay back down.

The hall fell silent as all the little animals practised breathing slowly and deeply. In no time at all, Peanut found himself drifting off to sleep to the sounds of a duckling softly snoring, a puppy gently grunting, and a guinea pig sleepily snuffling.

'It's time to slowly open your

eyes,' Dr KittyCat announced. 'Well done, everyone.' She climbed down from the stage.

'How are you doing, Willow?' she asked.

'I feel much calmer and more relaxed already,' the little duckling yawned.

Peanut flapped his ears to wake himself up. 'Do you think you'll be able to go on stage tonight?' he squeaked.

'I'll try,' Willow quacked.

'We'll be here to watch tonight's show and cheer you all on,' Dr KittyCat promised.

'And rescue anyone who needs rescuing,' Peanut added.

Chapter Four

Dr KittyCat and Peanut took their seats
in the front row of the audience.

The theatre lights dimmed.

Sage stepped into the middle
of the stage in front of the curtains.
'Welcome to Thistletown Talent Show,'
she announced, as the spotlight fell on
her. 'It's going to be a fabulous show,

and I have a quick joke to tell you before we get around twoo-whit . . .' Sage paused as the audience chuckled.

'What lesson do owls like best at school?' She shuffled her wings and blinked at the audience. 'Owlgebra!' she hooted.

Peanut laughed. 'Sage looks very calm and relaxed up there, doesn't she?' he whispered to Dr KittyCat.

'She's a natural performer,' Dr KittyCat meowed.

'And now,' Sage declared, as the laughter died down, 'clap your paws and wings for the first act—Clover the magic bunny!'

The audience gave a round of applause as the curtains opened to show a top hat in the middle of the stage.

'Ta-da!' Sage hooted as Clover jumped out of it, clutching a magic wand in his paw.

'For my next trick, I need an assistant,' Clover told the audience. Peanut stuck his paw in the air. Everyone clapped as Peanut made his way onto the stage and into the spotlight. He looked across the packed hall as Clover pretended to take a carrot out of his ear.

Everyone's watching ME! he thought. It was very exciting, but also quite scary.

'Now, it's time to enjoy a song from Posy the puppy,' Sage announced as Peanut sat back down next to Dr KittyCat.

'Ak-ak-ak!' Posy cleared her throat

and launched into her song. 'When you feel sad, don't cry or wail; jump up and down and wag your tail,' she howled untunefully. The little animals bounced up and down on their seats and joined in the chorus.

'Posy's a great performer,' Peanut squeaked, 'but she makes my ears hurt.'

'Thanks, Posy, for making me owl,' Sage commented seriously. Everyone roared with laughter. Posy gave a little bow and stood in the spotlight, wagging her tail.

'Our next performer is Willow the duckling,' Sage announced. 'Willow's going to do the web foot waltz.'

Everyone clapped their paws and wings, but the place in the spotlight stayed empty.

'Where is she?' Peanut squeaked. 'I hope she doesn't have stage fright again.'

There was an uncomfortable pause. The little animals in the audience looked at one another.

'Here she is!' The audience breathed a sigh of relief as Willow waddled slowly into the spotlight. She was wearing a beautiful long dress covered in sparkles.

The waltz music started, but Willow didn't move.

'She's frozen to the spot!' Peanut squeaked. 'Is she having another panic attack?'

'No,' Dr KittyCat meowed calmly. 'She's doing her relaxation exercises. Look!'

Peanut stared at Willow. The little duckling's eyes were closed and he could see her downy feathers gently rippling as she breathed slowly and deeply in and out.

Willow opened her eyes. 'Please, can you start the music again?' she quacked.

Peanut held his breath as the waltz music began again, but there was no need to worry. Willow gracefully held out her stubby wings and began to dance on her big webbed feet. Her lovely dress twinkled in the spotlight as she whirled and twirled round and round the stage. Then, just as she finished her final pirouette, she put her left foot down on her right foot and swayed dangerously. Peanut hardly dared to watch. But Willow flapped her stubby wings and managed to stop herself falling over. She gave an enormous beaky smile as she bowed.

The audience got to their feet and clapped and clapped.

'Well done, Willow,' Dr KittyCat cheered.

Willow looked down from the spotlight and bowed again.

'Thank you, everyone, and especially Dr KittyCat,' she quacked. 'You helped me conquer my stage fright!'

Chapter
Five

The audience was still on their feet,
clapping, when Peanut heard a raspy
voice in his ear.

'It's my turn to go on stage soon,
and my throat is really sore,' Fennel the
fox cub said in a hoarse whisper. 'Can
you help?'

Peanut thought hard. He

couldn't remember Fennel having the
vaccination against fur and feather flu!

'Did you have the flu vaccine?'
he whispered.

'No,' Fennel croaked. 'I had a
tummy ache that day, so I couldn't
go to the clinic.'

Peanut gave a tiny squeak. 'Eek!'

Dr KittyCat turned to him. 'What's wrong?' she meowed.

'Fennel has a sore throat and his voice is hoarse,' Peanut squeaked. 'Those are symptoms of fur and feather flu. He didn't have the vaccine!'

'Follow me!' Dr KittyCat grabbed her flowery doctor's bag and led Peanut and Fennel into the dressing room at the side of the hall.

'The whole of Thistletown is here tonight,' Peanut squeaked. 'If Fennel has flu, anyone who didn't have the vaccination will catch it from him. There will be an epidemic!'

'Don't panic, Peanut,' Dr KittyCat meowed. 'Fennel doesn't look ill, does he?'

Peanut took three deep slow breaths in and out like Dr KittyCat had taught him.

'I'm not going to panic,' he told her. 'I'm going to think this through like you always do.'

Dr KittyCat nodded approvingly. Peanut turned to the little fox.

'Do you have any tingles or aches and pains in your muscles?' he asked Fennel.

Fennel shook his head.

Dr KittyCat put a paw on Fennel's nose. 'Your nose is nice and cool and damp,' she remarked. 'I don't think you have a fever.' She checked Fennel's temperature with the ear thermometer, just to be sure. 'Apart from your throat, do you feel unwell at all?'

Fennel shook his head.

'Fennel looks bright-eyed and bushy-tailed, and he doesn't have a temperature,' Peanut squeaked. 'I don't think he has fur and feather flu after all. Phew!'

Dr KittyCat smiled. 'Now you need to find out what is really wrong with him,' she reminded Peanut.

'Fennel, have you been doing anything to make your throat sore?' he enquired.

'Only yodelling,' Fennel croaked. 'I've been practising yodelling all day. It's my act.'

'You've been practising a bit too hard, ' Peanut told him. 'You've strained your voice.'

Fennel's bushy tail drooped and he hung his head. 'How am I going to do my act if I've hurt my voice?' he whispered.

Dr KittyCat opened her doctor's bag and handed Fennel a little box.

'Suck on these throat pastilles,' she told him. 'They will quickly soothe your throat. You'll get through your performance if you only yodel half as much as you were going to. Then you must rest your voice as much as possible for a day or two afterwards.'

'And come along to the clinic to have the flu vaccine,' Peanut added.

'But it will be a really short performance if I only yodel half as much as I was going to,' Fennel mumbled unhappily with his mouth full of pastille.

Peanut thought hard. A picture popped into his head of a mountain goat yodelling in the Swiss Alps. The yodels were bouncing back off the mountains.

'What if your yodels echo off something?' he suggested. 'That would make your act longer. But there aren't any mountains to echo them back . . .'

'Someone could echo the yodel back!' Dr KittyCat exclaimed. 'They wouldn't need to be on stage with Fennel. They could yodel from offstage.'

'I'll do it!' Peanut squeaked. His whiskers twitched excitedly, as he found a costume backstage.

Fennel's ears pricked up. 'Brilliant!' he yipped. 'It's time for the act. Let's go!'

'And the next act,' Sage announced, 'is Fennel the yodelling fox cub!'

Fennel skipped into the spotlight and raised his muzzle to the roof.

'Yodel-ay-i-ooo!' he yodelled.

Peanut cupped his paws round his mouth.

'Yodel-ay-i-ooooooooooooooooo!' he yodelled back.

'Yodel-odel-odel-odel-ay-i-ooo!' Fennel called, cupping a paw to his ear.

Peanut raced round to the other side of the stage.

'Yodel-odel-odel-odel-ay-i-ooooooooooooooooooo!' he echoed.

Fennel's bushy tail swished as he whipped round with a look of surprise on his face.

'Ha, ha, ha!' the audience laughed.

This is fun! Peanut thought. Each time Fennel yodelled, he rushed to a different place to echo the yodel back.

He hid behind scenery, scampered to the very top of the curtains, and, finally, popped his head out from the trapdoor in the middle of the stage.

'Yodel-odel-odel-odel-ay-i-ooooooooooooooooo!' he called.

Fennel and the entire audience fell about laughing.

'Thank you, Fennel the yodelling fox cub, and Peanut the echo.' Sage clapped her wings as they took a bow in the spotlight. 'That was a hoot!'

Chapter Six

'Yodel-odel-odel-odel-odel-ay-i-
ooooooooooooo!' Peanut yodelled as he
skipped back to the vanbulance. 'That
was awesome!' he told Dr KittyCat.
'I've never been in the spotlight before!'

'I've never seen anyone take so
many curtain calls before,' Dr KittyCat
laughed. 'You were brilliant, Peanut!'

'I'm not surprised,' Dr KittyCat giggled. 'I'll teach you an exercise to help you unwind,' she told him. 'I'll do it, too; it's very relaxing. First you lie down and close your eyes and take five deep slow breaths in and out. Ready?'

'Ready,' Peanut squeaked.

'Wiggle your toes,' Dr KittyCat murmured. 'Squeeze them tightly and arch your foot. Hold it for 1 . . . 2 . . . 3 . . . 4 . . . 5 . . . seconds. Now relax.'

Peanut followed her instructions. 'My feet and legs have gone all floppy,' he commented.

'That's how they're supposed to feel,' Dr KittyCat purred. 'Squeeze in your tummy muscles. Hold your tummy in for five seconds, then let it go.'

'That feels good,' Peanut sighed.

'Now, pull your shoulder blades together,' Dr KittyCat went on. 'Count to five . . . relax.'

Peanut did what he was told.

'And finally . . . frown and wrinkle your nose and clench your jaw tight. Hold it . . . hold it . . . let it go. That's it. How are you feeling?' Dr Kittycat asked Peanut.

'My body feels relaxed,' Peanut squeaked, 'but I'm still not very sleepy.'

'Aren't you?' yawned Dr KittyCat below him sleepily. 'I have something breathed slowly and deeply. It was easy to imagine he was in a fragrant field of lavender with the sun shining in a cloudless summer sky. It made him feel lovely and warm and drowsy.

'Goodnight, Dr KittyCat,' he yawned. 'I'll be ready to rescue again tomorrow!'

The end

If you loved Willow the Duckling, here's an extract from another Dr KittyCat adventure:

Dr KittyCat is ready to rescue: Daisy the Kitten

This time Dr KittyCat is helping a little kitten called Daisy who's hurt herself at the Cupcake Bake. What could have happened?

'I need to put icing on my cakes,' Daisy wailed. 'But I can't do it. It hurts too much!'

'We'll make you better as soon as we find out what the matter is,' Dr KittyCat reassured her.

Dr KittyCat smiled up at Mrs Hazelnut and the little animals. 'Daisy is safe in our paws,' she told them. 'Please get on with making your cupcakes while we help her.'

Peanut turned to Daisy. 'Now, Daisy,' he squeaked. 'You told us about your cupcakes, but what Dr KittyCat really needs to know is exactly what part of you is hurting . . .'

Here are some other stories that we think you'll love!